THE ADVENTURES OF LONG ARM

Scholastic Children's Books
An imprint of Scholastic Ltd
Euston House, 24 Eversholt Street, London, NW1 1DB, UK
Registered office: Westfield Road, Southam, Warwickshire, CV47 0RA
SCHOLASTIC and associated logos are trademarks and/or
registered trademarks of Scholastic Inc.
First published in the UK by Scholastic Ltd, 2015

ISBN 978 1407 15698 9

A CIP catalogue record for this book
is available from the British Library.

Printed by CPI Group (UK) Ltd, Croydon, CR0 4YY
Papers used by Scholastic Children's Books are made
from wood grown in sustainable forests.

1 3 5 7 9 10 8 6 4 2

www.scholastic.co.uk

CHAPTER 1
A NOT SO TALL STORY

You're here for a superhero story, I guess?
Batman, the Hulk, one of that crowd?

Well … you're in the right
place. Except this is a
superhero story with a
difference.

Meet schoolboy Ricky Mitre.

Oh, and there is an angry
teacher called Mr Pinkerton, but
I'm afraid he isn't green.

So if you're still interested, make yourself comfy, strap yourself in and get ready for a brand new hero ... one who's going to be around for a loooooooooooooooooooong time.

The first thing you'll notice is that Ricky has two arms of equal length. That's because the picture opposite was taken five weeks ago, when he was testing his friend Simon's new invention – the HeadCopter Mark II™

Simon is Ricky's best friend, and he is a genius. That's a word bandied about too often these days, but with Simon it's completely true. He can recite the entire alphabet...

What, not impressed?

... backwards...

Still not impressed?

... in Russian...

Still won't admit it?

… while jumping on a pogo stick.

Yeah, beat that, clever clogs!

Simon also knows all the

ingredients in toothpaste and

he once taught his goldfish

how to dance like Lady Gaga.

Simon is always inventing

incredible things. Sadly,

the HeadCopter Mark II™ was not one his

greatest successes.

Poker Fish

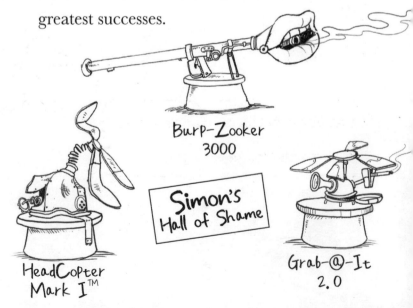

Burp-Zooker
3000

Simon's
Hall of Shame

HeadCopter
Mark I™

Grab-@-It
2.0

Ricky's dad was not happy that he had to take Ricky to casualty. He missed his favourite TV show, *Bottom Gear*.

It's a show all about motorized toilets hosted by three men with **BIG** bottoms.

Would you jump off a cliff if Simon told you to?

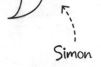
Ricky's dad

Erm...

Ricky

With some modifications, The HeadCopter Mark III™ should be fine for a cliff.

Simon

Having two broken arms isn't much fun.

- You can't play ZOMBIE CHASE

- You can't walk the dog properly...

STOP, ELLIOT!

- You can't turn the TV over when your Dad is watching his second-favourite programme, *Neil Or No Neil*. It's a game show where twenty-two men stand in a row but only one of the men is actually called Neil… Find Neil and win twenty zillion pounds.

Scarlett, Ricky's sister, isn't happy about the broken arms either. It means she has to help out.

But the worst thing for Ricky Mitre is not being able to play his favourite sport – basketball. Ricky absolutely loves basketball.

He dreams of basketball every night. . .

He longs to be on the basketball team at school, but there is a problem (besides the broken arms).

Ricky Mitre is only four feet and five inches tall, so he's got a lot of growing to do.

Being tall is not everything. There are good things about being short. For instance, low-flying birds are not a danger.

Hmm, what else? What else? Give me a

minute…

...

...

...

...

…Well, to be honest, that's about it.

CHAPTER 2

THE CASE OF THE MISSING CURRIED EGG SANDWICHES

Among all the other people unhappy about Ricky's broken arms, the unhappiest was his teacher, Mr Pinkerton. Mr Pinkerton had never liked Ricky Mitre since the day Ricky accidentally called him Mr Stinkerton. It was an easy mistake to make.

Mr Pinkerton was unhappy about Ricky's broken arms because it got Ricky out of PE. Though Ricky loved basketball, he hated PE – or "Pointless Exercise" as he called it. PE was second on Mr Pinkerton's List of Favourite Things (L.O.F.T.):

L.O.F.T. #2 - PE

Basketball was L.O.F.T. #1,552,101. Mr Pinkerton said team sports were for wimps. He believed in "self-improvement" through solitary exercise.

Also, without his arms, Ricky was unable to write lines, and Mr Pinkerton liked that too.

L.O.F.T. #3 - Giving lines to Ricky Mitre

Often, Ricky hadn't even done anything wrong, but that wasn't the point. He was just the sort of boy who got the blame. He had "one of those faces". Last year alone, Simon calculated Ricky had written close to two thousand lines. Here are a few of the more memorable ones.

I will not put a whoopee cushion on my teacher's chair.

Milk is for drinking, not pouring over Katie Locke's hair.

Butter is for spreading on bread, not in the corridor.

Ricky's casts remained on for five weeks, and in that time he couldn't get the blame for anything. After all, what trouble can a boy get up to without his arms? For five weeks, Mr Pinkerton was very grumpy.

Ricky's casts came off three days before his eighth birthday. The first thing he did was shoot hoops in his garden. Then he played ZOMBIE CHASE for three hours straight.

Then he decided to have a biscuit. Sadly, Scarlett had put the tin on the top shelf, out of reach.

The next day, Ricky was bouncing his basketball all the way to school, high-fiving everyone he came across. On the way, he saw a poster on a noticeboard outside the newsagent.

McRusty's Travelling Funfair
comes to Wolvesley!
Friday Only!
Fun 4 all the Family!

"Cool!" said Ricky.

Further up the street was another poster tacked to a lamp post.

Don't miss McRusty's!
Back by popular demand!
Health and Safety checked!
Rides and refreshments.

"Awesome!" said Ricky.

There was a third poster on the school gates.

No accidents this year!
Join us at McRusty's!
You will not get hurt!
We promise!
Don't believe the stories!

"I can't wait!" said Ricky. Thank goodness his casts had come off in time.

Simon was already in the classroom, working on some sort of drawing. He hid it in his desk when Ricky arrived.

"What's that?" asked Ricky.

"A surprise for your birthday," said Simon. "My greatest invention yet!"

"Is it the HeadCopter Mark III?"

"Even better!" said Simon.

The bell went for the morning's lesson, and Mr Pinkerton strode into the room. He put his curried-egg sandwiches in his desk drawer.

L.O.F.T. #1 - Curried-egg sandwiches

Mr Pinkerton's eyes lit up when he saw
Ricky's arms were back to normal.

"Right, everyone, maths books out!" he said,
rubbing his hands together.

The room groaned. No one liked
maths except for
Simon. He even
ate his dinner
mathematically.

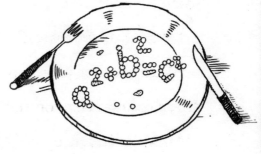

"We're having a
maths test on Thursday," said Mr Pinkerton.
"Everyone who passes gets to go to the
funfair. Anyone who doesn't …" he grinned
at Ricky "… can stay here."

"Don't worry," whispered Simon. "I'll give

you some coaching to make sure you pass."

As the lesson went on, Ricky began to feel sleepy. All the zombie chasing was taking its toll. His pen felt heavy and all the numbers swirled across his page. He couldn't keep his eyes open...

He dreamed he was playing in the NBA, dribbling around zombie players. Past one, past another...

The crowd were chanting.

He leapt for the net.

"MITRE!"

Ricky woke up with a jump.

"What is four times nine?"

Mr Pinkerton was standing in front of his desk.

"Pardon, sir?" said Ricky.

"What is four times nine?"

Everyone was watching him. Simon was waving his hands behind the teacher. Three fingers, then five on one hand and one on the other.

"Three hundred and fifty-one?" said Ricky.

Mr Pinkerton's face went red. "Three hundred and fifty-one?" he shrieked. "Of course it isn't! It's thirty-six, you imbecile!"

Then, as he often did when he was angry, Mr Pinkerton let out a little trump. Behind him, brother and sister Max and Meridon Foxtrot started to retch.

"I have to take a break," Mr Pinkerton said, edging towards the door. "Mitre – start writing lines. *I will not fall asleep in maths*. Thirty-six times. The rest of you, keep quiet!"

As soon as he left the room, Max staggered to the window and opened it. When it was safe to breathe again, Ricky went to the board to write his lines. Behind him, the rest of the class was anything but quiet. Paper aeroplanes were being thrown, Katie Locke and her inseparable best friend Rachel Quay (known throughout the school as Locke and Quay) were plaiting each other's hair and Nick Chalmers was busy tucking into his lunch box. Simon acted as a lookout by the door, until…

"Stinkerton's coming!"

And by the time he came back into the room, the class were back in their seats . . . and Mr Pinkerton looked a lot happier.

L.O.F.T. #4. Having a nice sit-down on the toilet.

And Ricky had written his line thirty-six times.

"Sit down, Mitre," said Mr Pinkerton. "And try to stay awake this time."

Ricky sat down and Mr Pinkerton took out the board rubber and erased the thirty-six lines.

"Right then, the nine times table," said Mr Pinkerton. "Let's carry..." He paused, his beady eyes fixed on his desk drawer. In two strides, he reached it and peered inside. His face went red. His nostrils quivered with rage.

"Mr Pinkerton," said Katie Locke. "There's a smell coming from Ricky's desk."

(Katie Locke had never forgiven Ricky for the milk-pouring incident. She had smelt like baby sick all day.)

Mr Pinkerton marched across the room and flung open Ricky's desk. The smell hit Ricky like a hammer. A hammer made of curried egg. Smeared all over his maths book were the remains of a sandwich.

"Oh, dear!" said Mr Pinkerton. But he said it in a way that didn't sound very upset at all.

Ricky didn't know how the sandwiches had got there. He wouldn't go near Mr Pinkerton's foul-smelling sandwiches without taking

serious precautions.

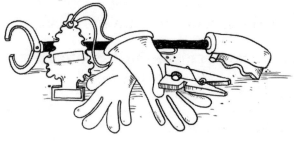

"It wasn't me, sir," he said.

Someone at the back of the classroom

chuckled.

"Of course it wasn't, Ricky!" said Mr

Pinkerton.

So who did steal the sandwiches?

Let's rewind. You heard that chuckle,

right?

Well, that horrible sneaky laugh belonged to Vince.

Vince is the sort of boy who sits at the back of the classroom and who everyone is scared of. Last year in the playground he threw a potato at a pigeon.

Vince is also the sort of lad who plays tricks and gets away with it. Tricks like putting a whoopee cushion on a teacher's chair...

Pouring milk on someone's hair...

And buttering the corridor...

But it was Ricky who'd been caught red-handed. So poor Ricky was accused, tried and convicted in the time it took Mr Pinkerton to blink his stink-eye.

"I've got a special punishment for you, Mitre," he said.

Something told Ricky that it would be a lot worse than writing lines this time. And he was right.

CHAPTER 3

THE DIRTIEST TOILET IN TOWN

When the bell rang for break time, the class
filed out. All except Ricky.

"Where do you think you're going, Mitre?"
said Mr Pinkerton as
Ricky tried to leave.

Mr Pinkerton
firmly hauled
Ricky down the
school corridor
until he reached

the door of the staff toilet. The caretaker, Mr Smears, was fastening a piece of paper to it.

"You don't want to go in there," he said, his face grey. "Something terrible has happened."

"I know!" said Mr Pinkerton, grinning. "I just used this toilet ten minutes ago."

Mr Smears shook his head in disgust. "I'm going to call in a specialist," he said. "More than my job's worth to clean *that*!"

"No need, Smears," said Mr Pinkerton, pushing Ricky torwards the caretaker. "Get this boy kitted out. He'll do the job."

Ricky swallowed. There must be some mistake. "Clean the toilet, sir?

"That's right, Mitre! You want to come on this trip to the fair, I assume?"

Ricky looked at the door, then at Mr Smears' pitying face, then at Mr Pinkerton again.

'Simple choice, Mitre," said his teacher.

Cleaning the toilet wasn't fair. Ricky wasn't even sure it was *legal*. But he had to go to the funfair. He just *had* to.

"I'll do it," he said.

"Excellent!" said Mr Pinkerton. "And remember, I want it SPARKLING!"

Five minutes later, Mr Smears arrived with a mop and bucket, as well as a small trolley

loaded with cleaning equipment. Mr Pinkerton
had already gone off to eat what remained of
his curried-egg sandwiches.

"Are you sure about this, lad?" said Mr
Smears.

"Yes," croaked Ricky, but he couldn't think
of any job he'd rather do less than cleaning Mr
Pinkerton's toilet.

Mr Smears patted him on the back. "Then good luck. If you're not out in an hour, I'll call a search party."

The caretaker scuttled away.

Ricky faced the door, took a deep breath and pushed it open.

The stench blasted over him and he staggered, feeling dizzy. He pushed the cart inside, clutching his nose. Ricky wondered what could have created such a foul odour. He hardly dared to look through the door of the toilet stall, and when he did, he looked away again quickly. There are some stains words cannot describe.

Ricky looked at the collection of equipment

and bottles in the cart. These would be his weapons. He readied himself for the battle ahead.

The problem was, Ricky didn't understand the labels on most of the bottles. There were lots of symbols that he didn't like the look of, but what did any of it mean?

After ten minutes of scrubbing, and at least a dozen flushes,

Ricky took a break. He thought about giving up. Perhaps if he begged Mr Pinkerton, he'd still be allowed to go on the trip to the funfair? Of course he wouldn't.

The problem was that the regular cleaner seemed to be having no effect at all. He'd need some sort of super-cleaner. The sort of thing used to clean up oil spills, or the stuff his sister Scarlett used to take all the layers of make-up off her face.

Simon would know what to do, of course. He knew all about chemicals and mixing them together.

But Simon wasn't here…

"Hmmm" said Ricky. "I don't need Simon. "Maybe I can just make my very own extra-powerful cleaning product. I'll call it 'Mighty Mitre'."

Ricky grabbed an empty bleach bottle from Mr Smears' trolley and headed off to the school canteen. He sneaked his way into the kitchen and opened the fridge. Inside he saw a giant vat of extra-extra, spicy-spicy BBQ sauce. "That'll do nicely," Ricky said, and he poured a little into his empty bottle.

He then turned around to see a cupboard labelled "Herbs and Spices". Ricky started adding to his bottle like he was a chef on

TV with a new cooking show called "Bang It All In". He added a pinch of paprika, a sprig of rosemary, a cinnamon stick, a dash of nutmeg and several shakes of hot chilli powder. He was going to add tarragon, but he changed his mind. No one likes tarragon. To finish he seasoned with salt and freshly ground black pepper, plus a squeeze of tomato purée.

Ricky rushed back to the staff toilet, stopping off at his locker on the way to get the extra-special ingredient ... a can of orangeade. But this wasn't any old can of orangeade. It was certainly the fizziest fizzy pop in the entire world. It was so fizzy that not only would it remove the enamel from your teeth in a matter of seconds, but research has shown if you put a cow in a glass of this orangeade and left it overnight, it wouldn't be there in the morning.

Ricky added the orangeade his concoction. The contents began to fizz, and orange-coloured, eye-watering, exotic-smelling smoke rose through the neck of the bottle. Ricky quickly ran back to the staff toilet.

He poured the whole bottle down the bowl, then pulled out one last ingredient from his pocket: a packet of popping candy. Into the toilet it went.

"Here goes," said Ricky.

He pressed the flush.

The liquid frothed, the popping candy popped louder than fireworks on Bonfire Night, and the water began to rise.

And rise...

"It's flooding!" said Ricky. "It must be blocked!"

Without even thinking, Ricky fell to his knees and jammed his hand into the bowl. The water reached his elbow, then his shoulder. Ricky wiggled his fingers around the U-bend, trying to find the blockage. If he flooded the toilet, Mr Pinkerton would probably make him write lines for ever!

Something gripped Ricky's hand. He tried to pull back, but couldn't. Panic almost stopped his heart. He was trapped!

He strained and strived, tugged and heaved, but something was holding his hand, deep around the U-bend. Strange green clouds swirled from the toilet. Sparks fizzed and flew around Ricky's head.

He felt his arm begin to stretch as the toilet sucked it deeper and deeper into the pipes.

This couldn't be happening. It must be all the
fumes making him imagine things.

Suddenly, whatever was holding his hand
vanished.

SLUUUUUUURRRRRP!

The water level began to drop.

Thank goodness! thought Ricky. He stood up, pulling his arm out of the toilet.

And pulling…

And pulling…

And pulling…

Ricky backed out of the cubicle, but still his arm was coming … and coming. A metre long, then two metres, then three. He stared in horror at his snake-like limb. Where would it end?

Where was his *hand*?

Was this some sort of dream?

Ricky reached the sink and gathered his new arm at his feet. He scanned up and down. It was at least five metres long! Finally, his hand, still wearing three marigolds, flopped out of the loo on to the wet floor.

The room began to spin.

Then Ricky fainted.

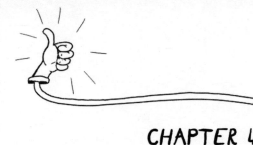

CHAPTER 4

IT'S A LONG STORY

"Ricky?"

Ricky Mitre was lying on something soft.

"Ricky? Can you hear me?"

Ricky opened his eyes, and saw Mr Smears standing over him, holding a wet cloth.

"Where am I?"

Mr Smears dabbed his head with the cloth and Ricky winced in pain. "I found you on the floor of the staff toilet."

Ricky sat up, and felt woozy. He was lying on a bed made of toilet roll in the caretaker's broom cupboard.

"What happened?" asked Ricky.

"You've grown a second head," said Mr Smears.

"But..."

"Just kidding. You've got a nasty lump, that's all. I drew a face on it because I was bored waiting for you to wake up.

But it's not your head you need to worry about," added Mr Smears.

Ricky remembered what had happened in the toilet.

"It's my arm, isn't it?"

Mr Smears nodded.

Ricky took a deep breath and looked across his body. His eyes went as wide as pancakes as they followed his arm from his shoulder. . .

… across the floor…

… along a shelf…

… around a bucket…

… along another shelf…

… over the lost property bin…

… to where it ended in a neat coil on the floor.

"Do you think anyone will notice?" he asked.

Mr Smears nodded. "It's likely, yes."

Ricky tried to move his arm, but he couldn't. It felt like a dead weight. He tried to wiggle his fingers, but his hand was as floppy and lifeless as a lifeless floppy thing. "What do I do now?" he asked. "I can't drag that around with me all day!"

"Maybe I should get Mr Pinkerton?" suggested Mr Smears.

"Maybe," said Ricky.

But as soon as Mr Smears had left, Ricky set to thinking.

If people found out about this, there was no saying what would happen.

The government might think he was an alien from the planet Skidillybop and experiment on him!

He had to keep it a secret. For now.

Ricky needed to hide his arm. He looked

around the room. There were paint pots on one of the shelves.

Perhaps he could paint his arm like a snake and pretend it was bring-your-pet-to-school day.

But that probably wouldn't work. The Animal Police might tranquillize him.

His eyes fell on a roll of bin liners. Extra strong.

Perfect! thought Ricky.

It took him a couple of minutes to load his arm into a black sack.

He crept to the door, and opened it. Mr Pinkerton was standing there.

"So what's this Smears tells me about an

accident? You've got a lump, I see."

"It's nothing, sir," said Ricky.

Mr Pinkerton frowned. "What's in the sack?"

"It's a long story," said Ricky.

"Well, you'd better get to the nurse," said Mr Pinkerton.

So Ricky followed Mr Pinkerton to the nurse's office, which was also the woodwork teacher's room – because, at Ricky's school, the nurse was also the woodwork teacher, Miss Chips.

"Can I help you?" she said, wiping sawdust off her brow.

"This lad's had an accident while messing

around," said Mr Pinkerton. He leant close to Ricky's ear. "One word about the toilet-cleaning, and you'll be writing lines until you're eighty!"

Mr Pinkerton left Ricky alone with the nurse.

She looked at Ricky's head. "Want me to take a bit off that lump with some sandpaper?"

"I think I'll be OK," said Ricky. "Can you call my dad to come and pick me up?"

Half an hour later, Ricky had managed to cram his arm into his bag when his dad arrived at the school gates in a sports car.

"What happened to our old car?" asked Ricky.

"Sold it for something more sporty," said his dad. "Three-hundred brake horsepower, zero to sixty in four seconds."

"Nice. But what about the Mitre annual camping holiday?" said Ricky. "It's only got two seats."

"We'll manage," said his dad.

CHAPTER 5
SOMETHING FISHY

At home, Ricky went straight upstairs. Elliot was sitting on his bedroom floor. Normally Ricky loved being off school, because he could play ZOMBIE CHASE or shoot hoops. But today he sat on his bed with his arm trailing across the floor. Elliot sniffed at it.

Ricky stared hard at his hand. It didn't matter how it had happened – somehow he had to learn to live with it.

"Move!" he told his hand.

His hand did not move. He couldn't
feel anything at all, even when Elliot licked
it.

Ricky went to his computer and did a one-
handed search for "arm-shrinking". Most of
the results were about how to make fat arms
thin by doing press-ups and only eating rabbit
food. Ricky didn't think that would work in his
case.

Ricky sighed and put
on some music. It was
his favourite band – the
Desert Penguins – and
their new song,
"A Coffee Boiled".

Ricky closed his eyes and let the music wash over him.

> *"A coffee boiled, is a coffee spoiled,*
> *I take a sip – and my voice is oiled!"*

Ricky began to tap the beat. *Tap-Tap-Tap.*

Elliot whined. Ricky opened his eyes. Across the room, his left hand was moving!

Ricky jumped off the bed, focusing on the feeling in his fingers. He told them to click, and click they did. He told them to stroke Elliot, and Elliot barked as the hand chased him around the room.

"It's working!" Ricky cried.

Then he heard footsteps on the stairs.

"Sweet pea!" called his mother.

Ricky's hand snaked across the
room and locked his door, just as
his mum turned the handle.

"Is everything all right in
there?" she said. "Dad said you
hurt your head at school."

"Just a minute!" said Ricky. He unlocked
the door, then shoved his hand and arm
down the side of his bed. His mum came in.

"Just having a lie down," said Ricky.

His mum turned down the music. "I'm glad,
sweet pea," she said. "It's dinner time – fish
stew!"

Ricky tried to smile, but it was hard. Even Elliot didn't like his mum's fish stew, and he would eat *anything*.

"I'm not hungry," said Ricky. "I think I have constipation."

"You mean concussion, sweet pea," said his mum. Her eyes went to his computer screen. "You're worried about your arms, dear?"

Ricky let his hand sneak across the floor and pull the plug from his computer. The screen went blank.

"Must be a power cut," he said.

"Well, you shouldn't worry, dear. Like your dad and I always say, you're a growing lad."

"If only you knew!" muttered Ricky.

By nine o'clock, Ricky's stomach was rumbling. He had an idea. He knew his mum and dad would be watching TV, and he could hear Scarlett on the phone in her room next door.

Ricky went to his window and reached out with his new arm. He felt his way along the gutter, then down the side of the house, and through the letter box. He let his arm feel along the kitchen cabinets, into the top cupboard where his mum kept all the good stuff.

"Dinner is served!" chuckled Ricky, gathering armfuls of biscuits, chocolate bars and crisps.

Ricky fell asleep a happy boy.

CHAPTER 6
A GREAT DAY AT SCHOOL

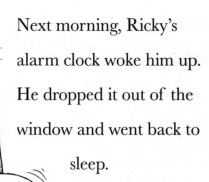

Next morning, Ricky's alarm clock woke him up. He dropped it out of the window and went back to sleep.

He woke again half an hour later to his mum banging on his bedroom door.

"Wake up, Ricky. Simon's here."

Ricky stumbled out of bed and went to the window, keeping his arm out of sight. Simon was standing on the doorstep.

"Coming to get the bus?" he called up.

"Er... I'll catch you up!" said Ricky.

Simon looked glum. "OK. See you at school later, then."

He walked away. Ricky grabbed his alarm clock out of the bush and checked the time. Eight o'clock!

Five minutes later...

... he was ready. But there was a problem. How could he hide his ridiculously long arm?

Ricky had an idea.

Ricky ran out of the front door, down the
street and around the corner, just in time to see
the bus leaving.

Time to hitch a ride.

He arrived at school on time, but his shoes had melted.

"Get some from lost property!" said Mr Pinkerton.

Ricky found Mr Smears reading a book in his broom cupboard.

"How's the arm?" asked the caretaker.

"Oh … fine," said Ricky. "Almost back to normal." He tried an unconvincing wave. "See! Have you got any spare shoes?"

Mr Smears rooted in the lost-property bin.

"These any good?"

"Not really."

"These?"

"Erm…"

"How about these?"

"Perfect."

Ricky made it to class and sat next to Simon.

"You're looking bigger," said his friend.

"I've been working out," said Ricky.

Mr Pinkerton eyed them all. "So, does everyone remember what is happening tomorrow?"

"My birthday!" said Ricky.

"It's the big maths test!" said Mr Pinkerton. "I hope you've all been revising. Remember – only those who pass the test get to go to the funfair on Friday."

Most of the class groaned. Apart from Simon, of course. He could pass a maths test blindfolded, his hands tied together and submerged in a tank of water.

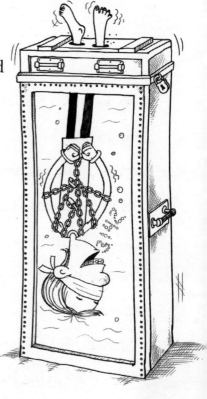

"What about them who don't pass the test?" asked Vince.

Mr Pinkerton smiled as his eyes swivelled on to Ricky. "Ricky can stay here," he said.

"Don't worry, Ricky," whispered Simon. "I'll come over later and help you revise."

"Ha!" said Mr Pinkerton, as if that was the funniest thing in the world. "If Ricky Mitre passes the maths test, *I'll* write lines."

Ricky wasn't going to let Mr Pinkerton get away with *that*!

As his teacher went to sit down, Ricky secretly shot out his arm under his desk and moved the chair.

SPLAT!

The whole class chuckled.

Mr Pinkerton stood up, frowning. He tried again.

SPLAT!

Mr Pinkerton dusted off his trousers. "Fine," he said. "I'll stand."

As he moved towards the board, he stumbled and fell flat on his face.

"Hey?" he said. "What's going on?"

Ricky grinned. "Sir, you've tied your shoelaces wrong."

Mr Pinkerton looked down at his feet. Sure enough, his shoelaces were tied together.

All the class were laughing now and Mr

Pinkerton's face was the same sort of red as a baboon's bottom.

"That's quite enough," he said, picking himself up again. "Let's get on with some spellings, shall we?"

Ricky snatched the board pen off his desk.

"Now where's my pen gone?" said Mr Pinkerton.

Ricky slid it into his back pocket.

"In your pocket, sir?" he said.

Mr Pinkerton found it. "Thank you, Ricky."

"My pleasure, sir," he replied with a wide grin.

Over the course of the day, Ricky's arm came in very useful…

…Especially at snack time.

In fact, Ricky had never enjoyed school so much.

As he was waiting for the bus that evening, he watched the cool kids playing basketball in the playground. They whooped, and jumped, and bounced, and chucked, and scored.

"Can I play?" asked Ricky.

The tallest of the basketball players spun the ball on his finger. It was Chad Mason, the captain of the school team. He had razor-sharp spiky hair that made him even taller still. People said he used a special hair gel made by scientists to keep buildings from falling down.

"'Course you can …" said Chad, holding out the ball.

But when Ricky tried to take it, Chad whipped it out of the way.

"… when you've grown as high as my waist!"

The whole team started laughing and high-fiving. Ricky felt his fingers tingling. He thought of all the things he could do.

But just then the bus pulled up. It was time to go.

"Shall I come over later and help you revise?" said Simon.

Ricky shook his head. "Don't worry about me, Si! I've got plans."

CHAPTER 7
A "CHAD" ANNOYING

Ricky had forgotten it was Wednesday, or as it's known in the Mitre house, "*Bottom Gear* Night".

Every Wednesday night, Ricky's dad would lock himself away in the living room to watch *Bottom Gear* whilst Ricky's mum would wander off to the garden shed to practise her Bikram yoga.

This meant that Scarlett was in charge.

Ricky sighed. Being in charge brought the worst out in his sister.

"Listen, pipsqueak," she said. "There's only one rule tonight. STAY. OUT. OF. MY. WAY."

"Suits me," said Ricky.

"I'm serious," said Scarlett. "I've got my boyfriend coming over."

"I didn't know you had a boyfriend," said Ricky. "Has he met you?"

"Leave me alone," said Scarlett, glaring. "I've only got two hours to get ready."

Ricky went into the garden with Elliot to practise with his basketball. He didn't miss a single shot.

It was seven o'clock when the doorbell rang.

Something green and sludgy appeared at

the back door. It took Ricky a moment to
realize it was his sister's face.

"He's early!" she said.

"What happened to your face?" asked
Ricky.

"What do you think happened to my face?"
asked his sister.

"Er?"

"It's a mud mask!" she screeched. "Let him in for me!"

"Sure," said Ricky.

When he opened the door, he was surprised to see Chad Mason. Chad Mason looked surprised to see Ricky too.

"What are you doing here?" asked Ricky.

"What are *you* doing here?" asked Chad.

"I live here," said Ricky.

"My girlfriend lives here," said Chad.

STOMP-STOMP-STOMP. Scarlett arrived at the bottom of the stairs and shoved Ricky out of the way. "Hey, Chad," she said.

"Remember what I said," Scarlett muttered under her breath. "No getting in the way, Tiny."

She took Chad's arm and dragged him inside. "Love your hair."

"Who doesn't?" said Chad.

Ricky didn't, that's who. He thought Chad's hair looked ridiculous. It was gelled even higher than usual, and brushed the ceiling.

Scarlett led him into the dining room.

Ricky went into the kitchen. *Perhaps I should try to be nice to Chad,* he thought. *If I want to get on the basketball team, I need to make him like me.*

He opened the door to the dining room.

"Can I get anyone a drink?"

Scarlett and Chad were giggling at the table. His sister glared at him. "What did I tell you about staying out of the way? It shouldn't be hard for you keep a *low* profile, after all."

"It's OK," said Chad. "I'll have a Coke, *Micky*."

"It's Ricky," said Ricky. Maybe Chad hadn't heard right – his ears were a long way up, after all.

He fished in the fridge and found a can of Coke.

"Thanks, *Nicky*," said Chad.

"It's Ricky," said Ricky. "With an *R*."

"Sorry, of course it is," said Chad, grinning as he opened the can.

He's making fun of me, thought Ricky. *But if I can just show him how good I am...*

"I've got a basketball hoop outside," he said. "It's my favourite sport."

"Is that right?" said Chad. "Maybe you want to be on the team? We've got a practice tomorrow, during PE."

"Yes, please!" said Ricky. "I could show you a few shots if you like."

"Sure thing, *Vicky*," said Chad. He was laughing so much a little bit of Coke spluttered out of his mouth.

"My name is *Ricky*," said Ricky. "I've told you three times!"

"I know," said Chad. "It's just I've got a bad *short*-term memory. Get it!"

Scarlett guffawed so hard Ricky thought she might cough up a lung.

Ricky balled his fists and ran out of room.

I'll show you, he thought.

CHAPTER 8
A TESTING BIRTHDAY

The next day was Ricky's birthday. His parents had bought him the latest computer game, ZOMBIE RUN, and a new basketball shirt with the number 8 on the front.

"Thanks, Mum and Dad!" he said.

His sister had made him a card and written a poem inside.

> Today you're only eight,
> But it's written in the stars, it's fate,
> That when you're older, beard and all,
> You'll still only ever be three feet tall.
> Happy birthday, "little" bro
> Scarlett x

"Thanks, sis," he muttered.

At school, Chad Mason and all his friends were already in the playground throwing around a basketball.

"Still planning to come for the tryout later?"

he called over to Ricky. "We need someone to look after refreshments."

Chad cackled.

Ricky ignored him, but when Chad wasn't watching, he sneaked a hand into his bag and took out Chad's most prized possession: his tube of hair gel. Grinning, Ricky went to see Mr Smears.

He knocked on the door to the caretaker's cupboard and there was no answer. He opened the door a fraction and peered inside. The caretaker's trolley was in there. Ricky quickly rooted around inside until he found what he was looking for. He was just leaving when Mr Smears appeared at his back.

"Can I help you, lad?" he said.

Ricky hid what he had borrowed in his pocket. "I just came to return these," he said, plucking the trainers out of his bag.

Mr Smears' wrinkled eyes bored into him. "You're sure you're not up to something?" said the caretaker. "You know, you've been given a gift, Ricky. You should use it wisely."

"You mean this?" said Ricky, nodding towards his long arm. "It's not a gift – it's a pain in the neck. Well, in the shoulder actually."

He hurried away. Time to put the plan into action.

"Happy birthday, Ricky," said Simon as Ricky came into the classroom. There was a box on his desk, in wrapping paper.

"For me?" said Ricky.

Simon nodded. "I've been working on them for ages," he said.

Ricky tore off the paper, and found a shoebox inside. He prised open the lid. Inside was a pair of red basketball boots – with a difference. They had metal tubes running down the side and into the soles, and each had a button near the toe.

"I'm calling them BolsterBoots," said Simon. "You just press these buttons –" He did so, and lights flashed up and down the sides of the boots "– and they let you jump twice as high as normal. *At least.*"

Ricky looked at the boots and felt an itch of irritation. Even Simon just saw him as a short person. Why did everyone always focus on his height? Just because he couldn't look in the bathroom mirror, or reach the coat pegs. He switched off the boots and placed them back in the box. "Thanks, Simon," he said, "but I don't need rocket boots."

"*Bolster*Boots," Simon corrected.

"I don't need them, either," said Ricky. "I'm going to get into the basketball team all by myself, you'll see."

"Oh," said Simon. "I just thought. . ."

Mr Pinkerton bounded into the room,

grinning from ear the ear, and bringing a wave of general egginess.

"Take your seats, everyone," he said. "It's maths test time!"

Ricky's stomach sank. He'd completely forgotten about the test. He'd been planning to revise the previous night, but after being humiliated by Chad and his sister, he'd just played ZOMBIE CHASE and gone to bed.

The whole class was silent as Mr Pinkerton handed out the test papers. They all wanted to go to the funfair.

Ricky turned over the paper and looked at the first question.

David has twice as many apples as Scott, and four times as many as Fred. If Fred has eight apples, how many apples are there altogether?

The words and numbers swam before Ricky's eyes. How was he supposed to work that out? Why did these kids have so many apples? Were they the children of greengrocers?

He looked sideways and saw that Simon was already scribbling an answer down. If only he had revised.

Looking up, he saw Mr Pinkerton watching him with a grin. "Happy Birthday," the teacher mouthed.

Ricky looked at the next question.

If I spend half my weekly pocket money on books and a quarter on stamps, I have £1.20 left. How much pocket money do I get in a year?

Ricky swallowed. What did that even mean? What normal kid spent their pocket money on stamps?

All ten questions were basically the same. All were impossible to understand. All were about weird children who ate too much fruit or had questionable hobbies. Simon, Ricky noticed, finished with five minutes to spare and put his hand up.

"Can I use the toilet please, sir?"

Mr Pinkerton nodded. "Make it quick."

Ricky was sweating. He hadn't answered a single question. The sheet in front of him was blank. If he didn't pass, he couldn't go to the funfair with everyone else. Glancing across, he saw that Simon had left his paper on the desk. A naughty thought wormed its way into Ricky's brain.

Go on ...
copy Simon's test ...
he won't mind.

He couldn't cheat!

Could he?

Mr Pinkerton was gazing towards his desk drawer, no doubt already longing for his curried-egg sandwiches.

Ricky would have to be quick. He let
his arm unroll beneath his desk and
his fingers scurry towards Simon's. He
snatched the paper off the desk. He looked
up to see Mr Pinkerton staring right at
him (at his face, not his arm). Ricky leant
closer over his test paper, pretending to
concentrate. Meanwhile, his arm went on a
little trip …

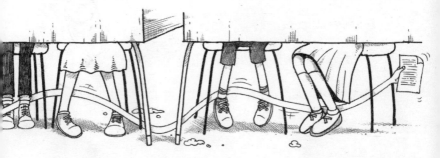

… to the staffroom.

Ricky felt his way to the photocopier, and made a copy of Simon's test paper. By the time Simon came back, Ricky had a full sheet of answers in front of him.

"Time's up," said Mr Pinkerton. "Make sure you put your names on the paper before you hand them in."

Ricky scribbled his name at the top of the page and placed it on Mr Pinkerton's desk.

"How'd you do?" asked Simon as they left.

Ricky shrugged casually, but inside his stomach was churning with guilt. "We'll see."

CHAPTER 9

FROM HERO
TO ZERO

But there were more important things to worry
about than the maths test. The next lesson was
PE.

Ricky changed into his new shirt, coiling his
arm beneath the baggy material.

"Sure you don't want the BolsterBoots?"
said Simon.

"Trust me, I won't need them," said Ricky.
"I've been practising."

As he strode out on to the basketball court,

everyone burst out laughing.

But not at Ricky – because standing in the
middle of the court was Chad Mason.

"What's going on?" said Chad.
"I don't understand."

"Is that some new dance
move?" asked one of his friends.

"My hands are STUCK!" said
Chad.

"Must be that gel of yours,"
said another boy. "I always said
you use too much."

"Yeah, must be," muttered
Ricky, fiddling with something
in his pocket.

Mr Pinkerton came out of the changing rooms in a tracksuit. "Yes, Mason?" he said.

"Sir, there's a problem," said Chad.

"Is that why you have your hands in the air?"

"That IS the problem, sir. They're glued to my hair."

"We'll get some scissors," said Mr Pinkerton.

"No!" said Chad. "I can't cut off my hair!"

Mr Pinkerton sighed. "Well, you'll just have to sit out the practice," he said. "We need a stand-in – anyone?"

Ricky shot up his hand high over everyone's heads and jumped up and down. "Me, sir!"

"Mitre – is that you?" asked Mr Pinkerton.

The rest of the players parted and Ricky puffed out his chest. "Just give me a chance, sir," he said. "I'll show you I'm ready to be on the team."

Everyone sniggered. "Very well," said Mr Pinkerton. "This should be very amusing, to say the least."

Well, you can guess what happened next, can't you?

Ricky Mitre played basketball like never before.

He dribbled…

And tackled…

And jumped…

And scored.

The rest of the PE class stopped to watch.
Mr Pinkerton was dumbfounded.

You see, the *normal* Ricky Mitre was pretty
good at basketball. He'd just never been given
the chance. But the long-arm version was
UNSTOPPABLE! Even Chad
Mason was impressed.

By the time Ricky left the court, he'd scored thirty-four baskets single-handedly.

"I think we have a new basketball captain," said Mr Pinkerton unhappily.

Eveyone clapped. Except Chad Mason.

And so, all was well. Ricky had enjoyed the greatest birthday ever. He was on the team and the next day was the McRusty's Funfair.

What could possibly go wrong?

The first clue that something was wrong was the huge grin on Mr Pinkerton's face the next morning.

"I'm pleased to say that most of you have passed the test," he said, as he began to hand out the papers. "But only two people got full marks. They were Simon. . ."

"Big surprise," said Vince.

". . . and our new basketball superstar, Ricky Mitre," said Mr Pinkerton.

Ricky tried to smile weakly.

"And for that reason," said Mr Pinkerton, "neither of them will be going to the funfair."

A series of gasps went around the classroom. Ricky felt the blood drain from his face.

"Why can't they go, sir?" asked a gleeful voice from the back.

"Good question, Katie," said Mr Pinkerton, holding up two pieces of paper. "Because they CHEATED."

Simon looked shocked.

"See the name at the top here?" said the teacher. "Do you SEE it, Ricky?"

"Yes, sir," said Ricky quietly. "It's my name."

"Indeed it is," said Mr Pinkerton. "But do you also see this name, here?" He pointed to the bottom of the paper, where Ricky read "Simon Evans".

"Ah…" said Ricky.

Mr Pinkerton tore both pieces of paper in two and dropped them on to the floor. "It's quite obvious to me what has happened here. Young Evans decided to leave the classroom for a supposed toilet break, but instead he went to the staffroom and made a copy of his own answers for his accomplice here. However, the pair aren't *that* clever because Simon had forgotten that he'd written his own name on the bottom of the paper before he photocopied it … and Ricky was daft enough not to notice."

"That's not true!" said Simon. He glanced at Ricky with a frown.

"Then please explain yourself," said Mr Pinkerton.

"I... I can't," said Simon.

"Anything to add, Ricky?" said their teacher.

Ricky's face burned. He couldn't look his friend in the eye. He couldn't think of what to say. If they found out about his arm, it was all ruined. He'd be off the basketball team. His life would be over. He wouldn't just be the vertically-challenged kid. He'd be the vertically challenged kid with the freakishly long arm. He couldn't let them all know.

"Nothing to add," he said quietly.

CHAPTER 10
FAIR PLAY

Later that afternoon...

McRusty's Travelling Funfair was the most exciting thing to happen to Wolvesley in a long time. *Wait a moment!* you're thinking. *What about the annual largest-puddle contest? What about the time everyone forgot Tuesday and skipped straight from Monday to Wednesday?*

In fact, McRusty's Travelling Funfair was the most exciting thing to happen since the last time

McRusty's Travelling Funfair came to town.

And that was exciting for all the wrong reasons.

McRusty's roller coaster ride, the Vomatron, had

lived up to its name. McRusty served five years

for gross negligence, but all his time behind bars

he was thinking up new ideas for his rides.

$$m_b = h_b = l_b = \sqrt{a^2 - b^2/4}.$$

$$d = \frac{\pi - \beta}{2}. \quad S = \frac{bh_b}{2} = \frac{a^2 \sin\beta}{2}.$$

$$S = a^2 \sqrt{3}/4.$$

And on the day of his release, McRusty set to work rebuilding his empire. The whole town agreed that McRusty's was bigger and better than ever. Children and their parents rushed to join in the fun.

There were a few problems with the rides. The dodgems didn't dodge.

The ghost train was a little unghostly due to pay cuts.

The carousel looked a little tired.

And the coconuts on the coconut shy didn't

like being looked at.

But the most impressive ride of all was Hailey's Vomit. Luckily, McRusty still had all the pieces from the Vomatron. He just had to put them all together again. He even found nearly all the bolts and screws.

Mr Pinkerton led the party of school children. "Stay close to me, all of you."

Vince had other plans. He didn't want to stay close to Mr Pinkerton, because of the lingering aroma of curried egg. So when Mr

Pinkerton went to the toilet…

CHAPTER 11
HiGH STAKES

Not everyone was having fun.

Back at school, Ricky and Simon were in detention. Specifically, they were in detention with Mr Smears, because all the other teachers were at the funfair. Mr Pinkerton had them writing lines.

I will not cheat in my maths test.

"I still don't understand," said Simon. "*I*

didn't photocopy my answers. My paper didn't leave the room."

Mr Smears looked up from his book, *A Mop in the Right Direction: A Caretaker's Brave Decision.* "You should tell him the truth, Ricky."

"What truth?" said Simon.

Ricky sighed. "I've been keeping a secret."

"Your middle name is Trevor?" said Simon.

"No," said Ricky. "Something worse than that."

"Nigel?"

Ricky shook his head. "I copied your paper," he said. "But I didn't leave the room to do it."

"How?" asked Simon.

Ricky showed him. "That's how."

Simon looked impressed. "Is that from doing weights?"

Ricky explained what had happened on the fateful day his arm became trapped around the U-bend.

"I'm sorry," he said. "I should have told you earlier."

"So why didn't you?" asked Simon. "I'm supposed to be your best friend."

"I don't know," said Ricky. "I suppose I was scared at first, then I got a bit carried away."

Simon frowned. "Is that how you got on the basketball team as well?"

Ricky felt his face go crimson. "Yup."

Mr Smears shook his head. "I told you, Ricky – you should use your gift to help others."

"I know that now," said Ricky. "But who needs a stupidly long arm?"

Meanwhile, back at McRusty's, Mr Pinkerton was still trapped in the loo, trumping angrily.

Scarlett, Chad and the basketball team had reached the front of the queue for Hailey's Vomit.

"I heard it pulls 10Gs," said Chad. "That's enough to break your neck."

"Better be careful, then," muttered Chad's friend Brett. "It might be enough to move your hair out of place too."

They all climbed on, and McRusty went through the safety procedures.

"Belts on, keep your hands inside, no eating or drinking … and here's your complimentary barf bag."

"Ready?" said McRusty.

"Ready!" they cried.

"Prepare for Orbit!"

McRusty pushed the lever, and the cart set off, rattling along the tracks.

Up and up it climbed. Then up some more.
It wasn't known as the highest roller coaster in
the world for nothing.

What could go wrong?

As the cart thundered and rattled and
swerved and looped, 11,348 screws held
firm.

One, unfortunately, did not. This one.

As the cart shot around a loop, the screw
snapped and two sections of track came
apart. In a shower of sparks and with a
screech of metal, the cart veered off the
rails. Scarlett gasped. Vince squealed. Katie
Locke shuddered. And everyone closed their
eyes and hoped for a miracle.

CHAPTER 12
SUITED AND BOOTED

Back at the school, detention dragged on and on. It felt like a lifetime.

But Ricky heard a noise. "What's that?" he said.

Simon opened the window. "It sounds like a siren. And not just one."

Ricky and Mr Smears went to the window too, just in time to see three fire engines, two ambulances and a police car zooming past.

"They're heading to the fair!" said Simon.

"Something terrible must have happened!"
Mr Smears switched on his radio and wiggled
the dial.

"*… have reports just in that there's a situation at
McRusty's Travelling Funfair. Witnesses say that there
are people trapped at the top of a roller-coaster ride.*"

Simon and Ricky gaped at each other.

"*… apparently a runaway cart is suspended
some hundred feet in the air. Too high for emergency
services to reach, even with their longest ladders…*"

Ricky gritted his teeth, and his eyes travelled
the length of his arm. "I can save them," he
said. "But only with your help."

Ricky turned to his friend, "I'm sorry I
didn't tell you about my arm, Si. You're right,

you're my best friend and best friends tell each other everything. It won't happen again, I promise."

Simon smiled. And then realization hit. "But … you can't help! Everyone will see your arm."

Ricky stroked his chin. Simon was right, as always. What he needed was a way to use his arm, but stay hidden. He pointed to Mr Smears' cart. "Have you got any light bulbs in there?"

Mr Smears fished one out. "Why?"

"Because I need a light-bulb moment," said Ricky.

And as soon as his fingers touched the bulb, an idea sprang into his head.

"I'll wear a disguise!"

Mr Smears smiled. "And I know just where you can find one – the lost property box."

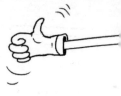

Ten minutes later…

Ricky searched high and low for the right costume. The perfect blend of heroic and functional. If he was going to save the day, it would be in style.

And this is what he came up with…

"You've got no shoes," said Mr
Smears.

"Nothing fitted," said Ricky.

Simon had a solution.

"Try these!" he said, handing
Ricky the rocket boots.

Ricky pulled them on. "They fit perfectly.
How do they work?"

"Just twiddle your toes," said Simon.

Ricky did, and he shot straight into the ceiling.

"Twiddle less," said Simon.

Ricky gathered up his arm. "To the funfair!" he cried.

CHAPTER 13
NEWS TRAVELS FAST

The people of Wolvesley were glued to their television screens. Not literally. That would be strange.

They were watching the report from McRusty's Funfair. So no one saw Ricky Mitre shooting past their windows on his rocket boots. As he neared the roller coaster, he saw the cart hovering perilously over the ground.

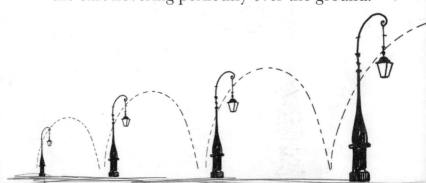

The people inside saw him too.

"Is it a bird?" said Brett.

"Is it a plane?" said Chad.

"Obviously not," said Scarlett. "Are you both blind? It's a really short, badly dressed Superman."

Ricky landed behind the line of fire engines and the ambulances and the police car. Everyone was standing around, wondering what to do. Apart from Mr Pinkerton. He had

finally escaped the toilet
after two hours and was
now lying down, being
treated for the fumes.

"Who's in charge
here?" said the Chief
Constable. "Where's the fair manager?"

People looked around for McRusty, but he
had long gone.

Up above, the cart's nose tipped a little.
Scarlett screamed, and everyone on the
ground let out a gasp.

"It's going to fall!" cried the policeman.

Ricky knew he couldn't wait a moment
longer. "Stand back, everyone!" he said, in the

deepest voice he could manage. He strode
into their midst, and unfurled his arm. The
crowd stared in amazement. He reached up
and up and up, until his hand touched the
side of the cart.

He tried to push it back on to the track, but he didn't have the strength.

"It's no use!" said the reporter.

Ricky seized a megaphone and spoke to the people in the cart.

"Use my arm to climb down!"

Scarlett trembled. Brett shuddered. And Chad clamped shut his eyes.

"You can do it!" cried Ricky. "It's your only chance."

Scarlett was the first to stand up. As she did so, the cart wobbled. "Come on, you lot," she said. "We can't sit around here all day."

Gingerly, she clambered out of the cart and

grabbed Ricky's arm. On the
ground, he gripped as tightly
as he could. "One at a time,"
he called. "I can't take you all!"

However, the people in the
cart didn't listen. Now they'd seen
Scarlett on her way, they all
jumped on to Ricky's arm, and
began to make their way down.
Ricky could barely hold on.

But, one by one, they made it
to safety.

The rescued passengers
rushed around Ricky
thanking him and slapping

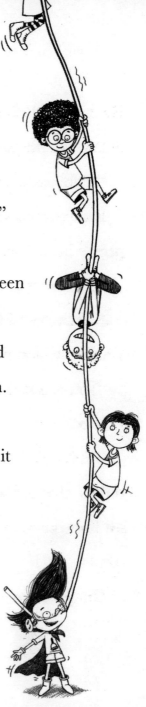

his back. All except one…

You forgot about Chad, didn't you?

Well, he was stuck in the cart, unable to open his safety-belt, because his hands were still glued to his head.

Ricky reached inside, fingers feeling for the safety catch. *CLICK!* Chad was free, but he still couldn't climb down.

"You'll have to balance, Chad!" said Ricky.

Chad edged on to Ricky's arm. Ricky tensed his muscles, desperate to keep his arm steady. One step at a time, Chad began to descend.

But when he was halfway, a gust of wind picked up. It caught Chad's hair like a sail.

He wobbled left, he wobbled right…

The crowd held their breaths …

… and then Chad fell.

CHAPTER 14

THE END OF THE BEGINNING

"Nooooo!" yelled the crowd, closing their eyes so they didn't see the splat.

"Nooooo!" wailed Scarlett, who was wondering what it would be like to have a splat for a boyfriend.

Nooooo! thought Chad, who worried about his hair being splatted.

But Ricky saw something in the sky. Something swooping with incredible speed.

It couldn't be…

…but it really was.

In a blur, Simon caught Chad mid-air and carried him away.

The HeadCopter Mark III! thought Ricky. *He did it.*

Unfortunately, Simon realized, the HeadCopter Mark III was designed only to bear the weight of one person. He made it  about twenty metres, then both he and Chad plummeted from the sky.

Ricky panicked and looked around to see if he could help in any way.

Then he spotted it, right across the other side of the funfair.

"McCrusty's Semi-Inflated Bouncy Castle!"

Ricky threw his arm across the funfair and dragged the bouncy castle so it was directly under Simon and Chad, catching them as they fell.

"Bullseye!" shouted Ricky. He then quickly hauled Simon away. "We'd better get back to detention!"

No one noticed Ricky and Simon slipping away. Before long, people were munching their candyfloss, crashing their dodgems and queuing for Hailey's Vomit once again.

In the weekend that followed the fair, many things happened...

The police caught up with McCrusty. He was living in the Arctic with an Inuit family.

The press searched for the mysterious hero of Wolvesley. But try as they might, they couldn't find him.

Chad's mother, tired of doing everything for him, insisted he had his hair cut. Scarlett dumped him.

Ricky and Simon finally conquered the last level of **ZOMBIE RUN**. By Monday, everything was back to normal.

Everything except the length of Ricky's left arm. For Ricky Mitre, life would never be the same again.

Ricky now knew that his arm was meant to do good. There would be challenges ahead, mountains to climb and high cupboards to reach.

Ricky Mitre might still only be four feet five inches tall. But it didn't matter because from that toilet cleaning moment…

ACKNOWLEDGEMENTS

Firstly we'd like to thank our lovely agent, Grainne, for getting us a meeting with the publishers of this book.

Thank you to everyone at Scholastic, especially Maya and the two Sams.

Aleksei Bistskoff – your illustrations are perfect.

Thanks to Michael Ford for helping us with the writing process.

To Chris Parr: thanks, mate, for helping us out

in the early days of Long Arm.

Thanks to our mate Ed Thomas for being the one who told us that Long Arm would make a good children's book character ... you were right.

And finally thank you to you – you who is reading this right now, you who spent your pocket money and went out to buy this book. We really appreciate it and hope you like our little Long Arm journey.

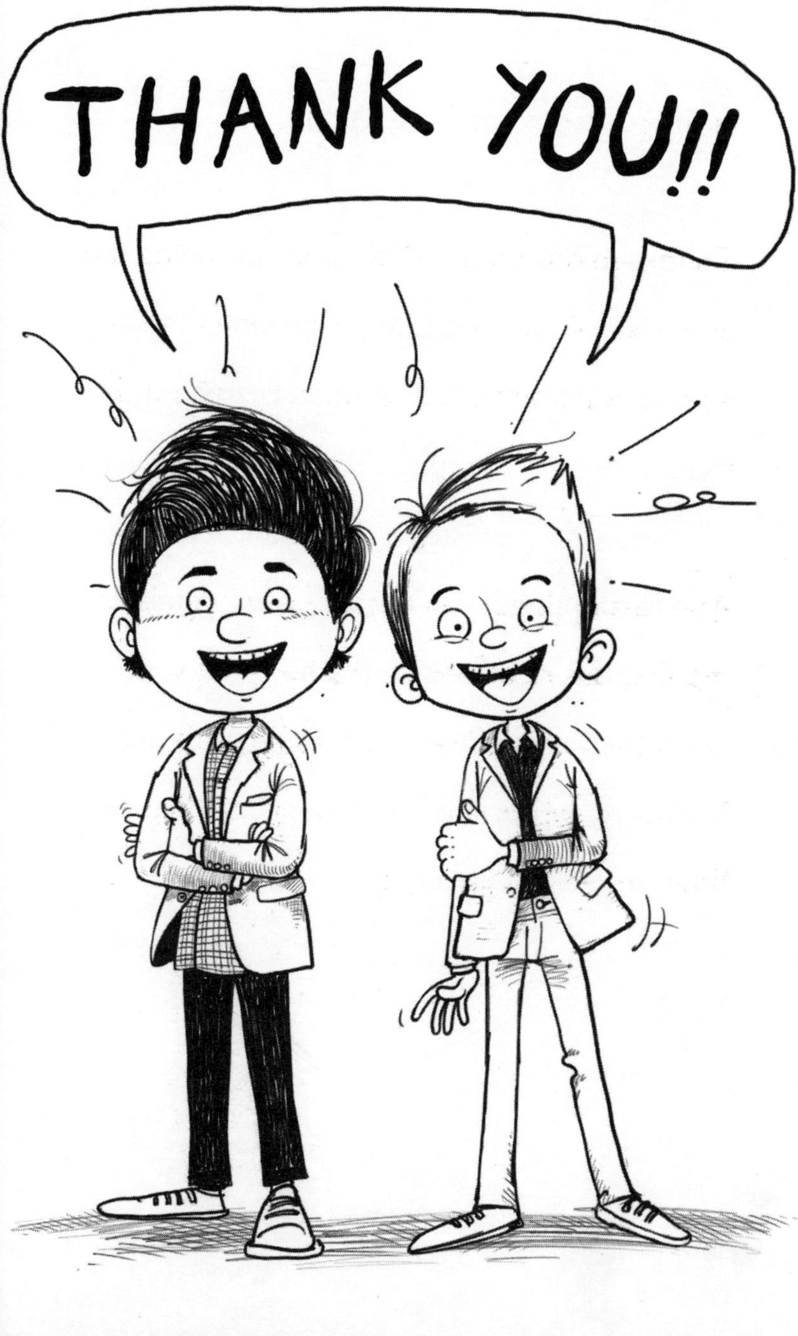
THANK YOU!!

After his first adventure with an extra-long arm, Ricky asked authors Sam and Mark some very important questions. Read on to discover what superpower they'd want, what their worst punishment would be and more!

LONG ARM

1. If you could have a superpower, which one would it be?

SAM It would be great to be invisible. You could spy on the bad guys and know exactly what they are getting up to.

MARK I would choose the power of invisibility so if you have to do your homework at least you can pop into the kitchen and get snacks without your parents seeing.

2. What about your superhero name, what would yours be?

SAM Dave.

MARK "The badger" because they look cunning and I reckon you could make a really cool suit that looks like a badger.

3. If you had a superpower would you use it for good or to play pranks?

SAM A bit of both. I'd definitely spy on Mark.

MARK Maybe pranks on people you find annoying, but overall I would like to be a good guy that saves the day.

4. If you had a long arm what would be the first thing you'd do with it: hitching a lift to school, sneaking food from downstairs or something else?

SAM I would become very lazy and stay in bed all day and just use my arm to do everything.

MARK Maybe see how many one-armed press-ups I could do.

5. Cleaning the staff toilets is a pretty bad punishment. What would be the worst punishment you could be given?

SAM People would see this as a treat not

a punishment, but, if I was made to go on a

roller coaster all day; I hate them!

DON'T ... LOOK ... DOWN!

MARK   Going into dinner last because

you're left with the rubbish food.

6. My best friend Simon is a genius and loves inventing things. What do you wish you'd invented or what do you want to invent?

SAM I like things that are really simple but really useful. I wish I'd invented the zip. So many items all over the world use a zip.

MARK The see-through toaster as I'm always burning mine.

Are you the UK's funniest friend?

We're on the hunt for the UK's funniest friends! If you think that could be you and your best friend then simply head to **www.scholastic.co.uk/longarmbook** to enter the free competition*!

One lucky winner and their friend will win:

- The chance to meet Sam and Mark at an event at their school
- Their names in the second book in The Adventures of Long Arm series, out in 2016
- A signed copy of The Adventures of Long Arm
- £50 of funny books for their school

The competition closes at midnight on 31st December 2015.
*T&Cs apply — visit www.scholastic.co.uk/longarmbook for full details

Loved The Adventures of Long Arm?

Then why not visit the Long Arm website
where you'll find loads of fun things!
Head to www.scholastic.co.uk/longarmbook for:

- Superhero downloads

- Brilliant competitions

- Videos of Sam and Mark talking
about the inspiration behind the book

- All the latest news about
The Adventures of Long Arm